S0-AXA-540

LOST

Alexandra Mîrzac

TATE

Cat used to think he was the luckiest cat in the whole world. He had everything! Loving parents, a cosy home and lots of sunny places to sleep.

His parents were the best playmates a cat could wish for. And they were brilliant hunters – every week they would bring home fluffy balls and toy mice!

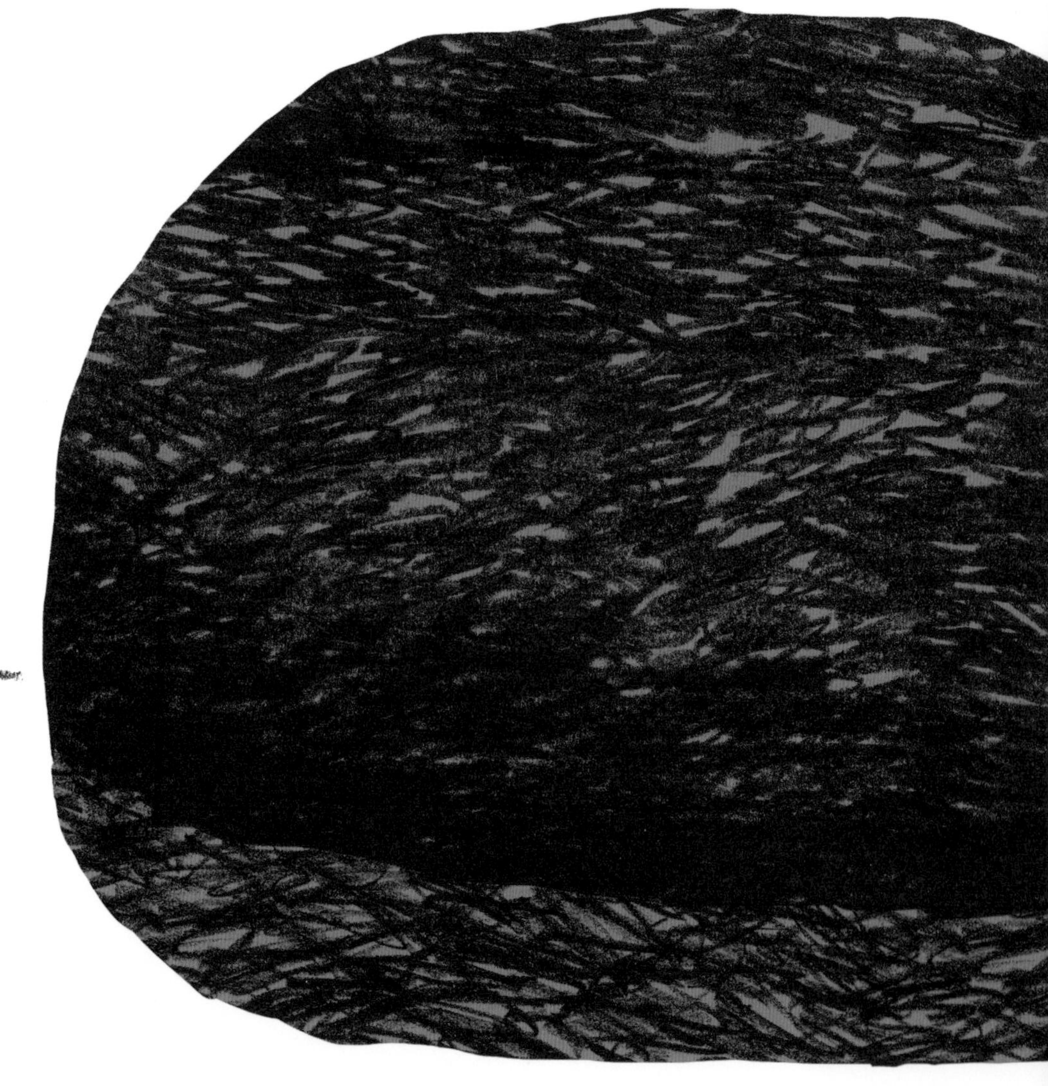

But lately it seemed that they preferred to play alone.

A thought started to grow in Cat's mind.

"Maybe they aren't playing with me
because they can't see me . . .

maybe I am INVISIBLE!"

Cat felt sad. He pictured a lonely life, with no one to love him, no one to care for him and no one to PLAY with him.

He decided to venture into the city . . .

hoping to find someone to play with.

He meowed,
and he purred,
he scratched
and he pawed.

But no one seemed
to notice him.

As he travelled further and further from home he started to worry.

Was it true?

Could he REALLY be invisible?

"That's it!" he thought. "I'm definitely invisible and no one is looking for me."

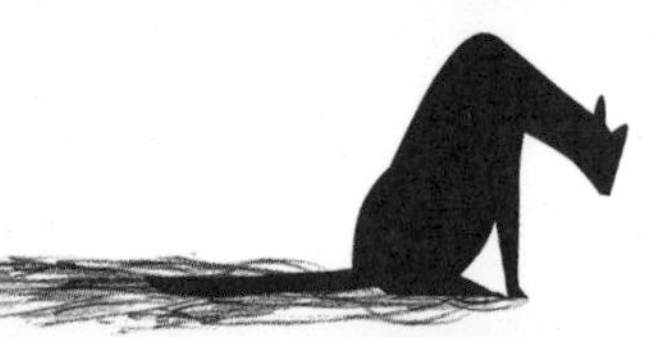

"Oh no!" Cat sighed. "Not only am I invisible, I am also LOST!"

Feeling tired and just a little bit sorry for himself, Cat decided to rest for the night.

He found an old tin of sardines for his supper and an empty cardboard box to sleep in.

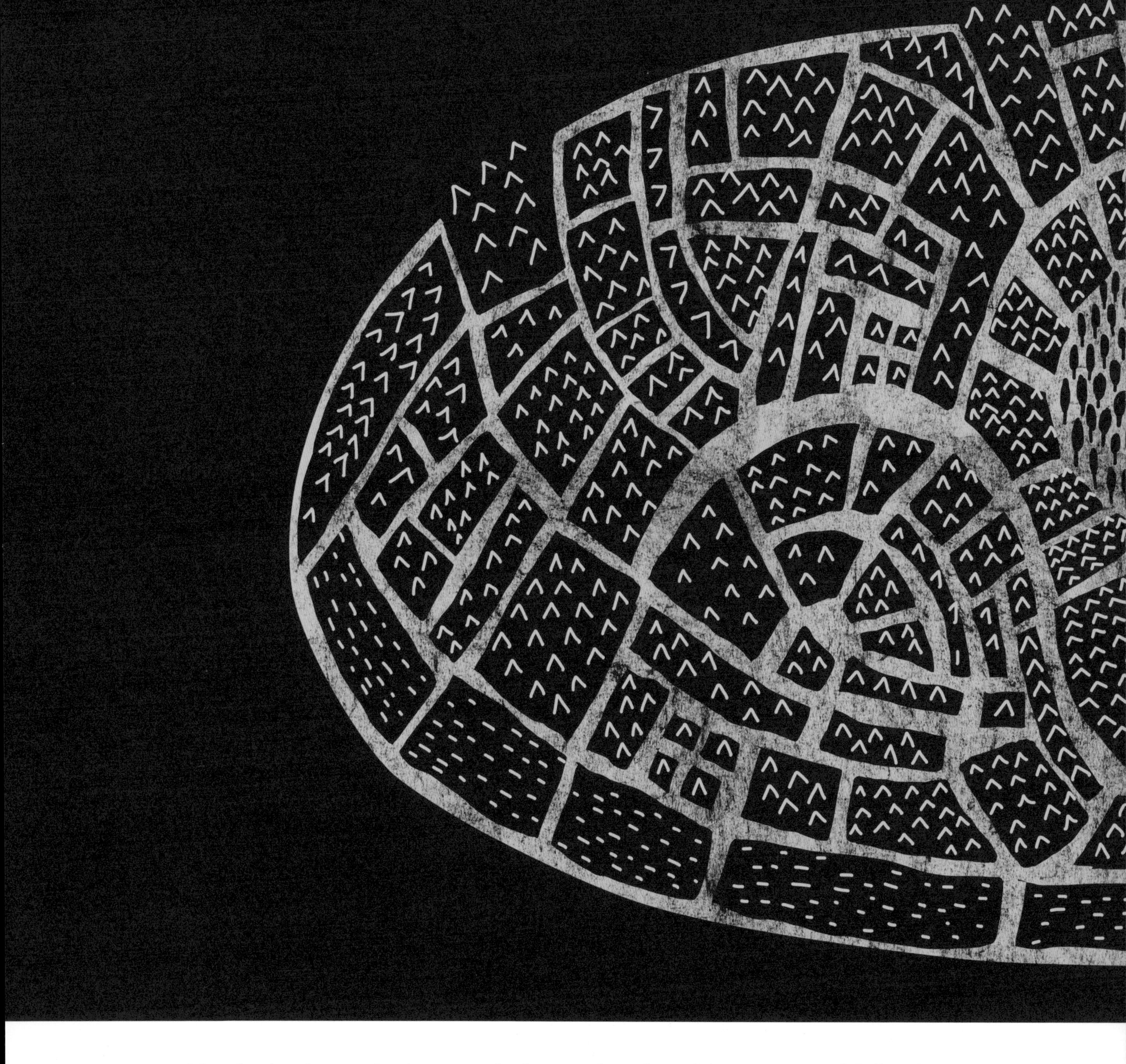

He climbed into the box, curled up tight, closed his eyes and fell asleep.

And then he began to dream . . .

He dreamed of lazing in his special spot in the sunny garden at home.

He dreamed he felt
a pair of kind, warm
hands pulling him close
for a cuddle . . .

He began to realise it wasn't a dream! He wasn't invisible.
He wasn't even lost anymore. Now he was . . .

FOUND!

From that day on, Cat and his parents made sure they did lots of playing together.

There were cuddles and strokes
and ear tickles galore!

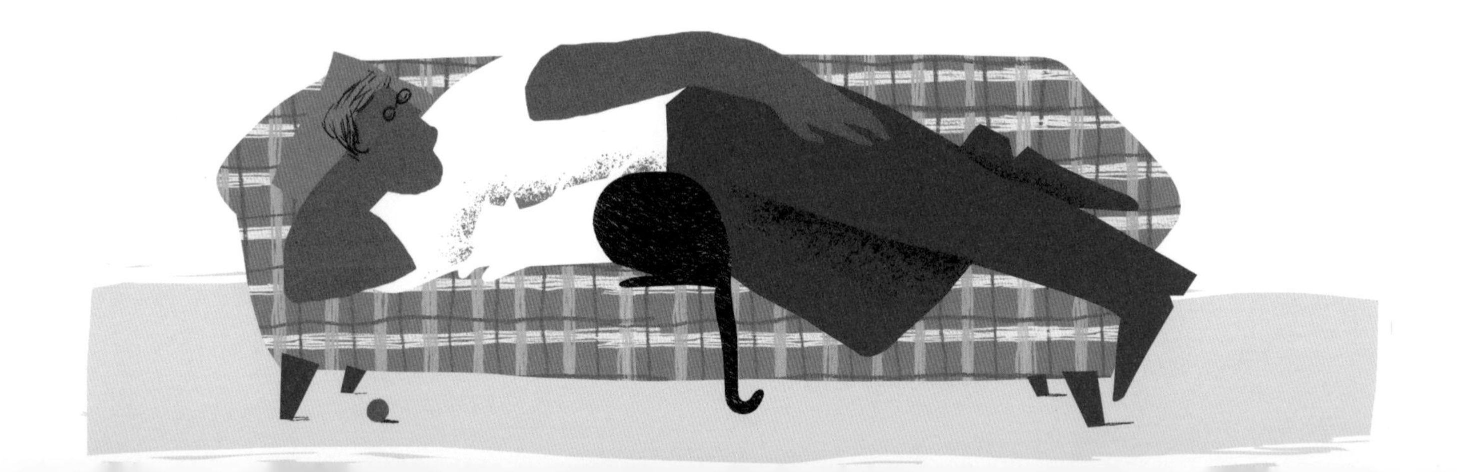

And Cat knew that even if he got lost again, there would always be someone who would come and find him.

Dedicated to Brutus.
The cat who inspired this story.

First published 2020 by order of the Tate Trustees
by Tate Publishing, a division of Tate Enterprises Ltd,
Millbank, London SW1P 4RG
www.tate.org.uk/publishing

A catalogue record for this book is available from the British Library
ISBN 978 1 84976 733 0
Distributed in the United States and Canada by ABRAMS, New York
Library of Congress Control Number applied for
Colour reproduction by Evergreen Colour Management Ltd
Printed and bound in China by C&C Offset Printing Co., Ltd

N
S